JR. CHAPTER BOOK

THE
BAILEY SCHOOL
KIDS

JR. CHAPTER BOOK

THE
BAILEY SCHOOL
KIDS®

DRAGONS DO EAT HOMEWORK

by Marcia Thornton Jones and Debbie Dadey
Illustrated by Joëlle Dreidemy

SCHOLASTIC INC.
New York   Toronto   London   Auckland   Sydney
Mexico City   New Delhi   Hong Kong   Buenos Aires

To Chris Rabold—A number one reading dragon who
knows the importance of reading, writing, and
inviting authors to meet the students in her district.
Read on!—M.T.J.

In memory of James Frank Smith—
a man who filled a room with mischief and fun.—D.D.

To Lisa and Camille, who would be very happy
to know dragons were eating their homework!—J.D.

ISBN - 13: 978-0-545-00234-9
ISBN - 10: 0-545-00234-6

Text copyright © 2007 by Marcia Thornton Jones and Debra S. Dadey.
Illustrations copyright © 2007 by Scholastic Inc.
All rights reserved. Published by Scholastic Inc.

SCHOLASTIC, THE BAILEY SCHOOL KIDS, and associated logos are
trademarks and/or registered trademarks of Scholastic Inc.

17 16   14/0

Printed in the U.S.A.
First printing, September 2007

CONTENTS

1

HOWIE

"Do I have to go in there?" Eddie asked. His friends Liza, Melody, and Howie stood beside him in front of Bailey City Elementary School.

Melody patted Eddie on the shoulder. "Don't worry. There are no monsters or aliens in there."

"Oh, yes, there are,"
Eddie said. "They're called
TEACHERS!"

"Teachers aren't monsters,"
Howie said. "They help us learn
things."

Liza nodded. "School is
fun."

Eddie stomped his foot. "Bike riding is fun. Swimming is fun. Video games are fun."

"Playing soccer is fun," Melody added.

"But school is not fun," Eddie said. "It's as icky as spinach!"

Howie shook his head. "There is one good thing about school."

2

YEAH, SCHOOL!

"What could possibly be good about school?" Eddie asked.

"I like spelling," Liza said.

"Yuck!" Eddie said. "The letters always get mixed up in my head. It's like the Attack of the Killer Words!"

"I like math," Melody told Eddie.

"Math!" Eddie screamed. "I get itchy just thinking about math. I am allergic to math."

Liza giggled. "You can't be allergic to math."

"I hope we learn how to multiply this year," Howie said.

Eddie scratched his arm. "I'm feeling itchy already."

"I like math and spelling, too," Howie said. "But the very best part of school is… homework!"

Eddie took one look at
Howie and fell flat on the ground.
It was true. Howie
loved homework.

He would rather
read than watch TV.

He worked on
math problems
instead of playing
video games.

He did science
projects just for fun.

3

OAK TREE

Where's Howie?

A few weeks later, something very strange happened.

Liza, Melody, and Eddie were waiting for Howie under the giant oak tree on the playground. It was their favorite place to meet before school. A chilly fall breeze was knocking leaves off the tree. "Where's Howie?" Liza asked as she zipped up her jacket.

"Howie is NEVER late for school," Eddie said. "See? There he is now."

Howie was walking slowly across the playground. His sweatshirt was torn. Leaves and twigs stuck out of his blonde hair. Mud covered the knees of his jeans.

"What happened to you?" Melody asked.

Howie looked at his friends. "You're never going to believe me," he said, "never in a million years."

4

MR. ZEP

Just then, the school
bell rang.

"Hurry, or we'll be late,"
Liza said.

Melody,
Liza, and Eddie
dashed for the
door. Howie
didn't run. He
didn't jog. He
didn't hurry at
all. He walked
like he was in a
dream.

Their teacher started every morning exactly the same way. Mr. Zep waited for everyone to get settled. He always had to wait for Eddie the longest.

Then Mr. Zep said, in a very quiet voice, "Please pass your homework to the front of the room."

Kids pulled papers out of book bags.

They grabbed pages from inside their desks.

They tugged papers from their notebooks.

They even dug into their pockets.

"Howie?" Mr. Zep asked. "Where is your math homework?"

Everyone looked at Howie. His freckles stood out on his pale face as he answered in a shaky voice.

"I...I...I...don't have it," he stammered. "A dragon ate my homework."

5

DRAGON?

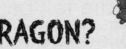

"What?" Liza gasped.
"What?" Melody asked.
"WHAT?" the rest of the
kids shouted. Howie always had
his homework.

Then the whole class laughed. Even Liza giggled. Eddie fell on the floor and rolled around. He laughed so hard his belly hurt.

"It's not funny," Howie said. "I was taking a shortcut through the woods this morning. Something swooped down and snatched it right out of my backpack. It was a dragon. I know it was!"

"You have to admit that your story is crazy," Melody said. "It's like saying an octopus stole your lunch money."

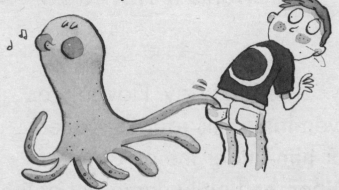

"Or a mermaid spilled your milk," Liza added.

"Even I know there are no such things as dragons," Eddie said.

Nobody believed Howie.

6

NO-HOMEWORK KING

The next day, Howie was even later. His friends waited for him under the oak tree. When he finally came out of the woods, he didn't say a word.

Leaves stuck out of his hair. Mud caked the knees of his jeans. He dragged his backpack on the ground behind him.

"What's wrong with your backpack?" Eddie asked.

"It got burned," Howie answered as he walked past his friends, "by a sneezing dragon."

When Mr. Zep asked for his spelling homework, Howie shook his head. "I don't have it," he said. "The dragon ate it again."

Every day that week, the same thing happened. When Mr. Zep asked for Howie's homework, he said, "The dragon ate it."

"This is crazy," Melody said to Howie one day after school. "You love homework."

Liza nodded. "What's wrong, Howie? Why aren't you doing your homework?"

Eddie took off his baseball cap and tapped Howie's head.

"I crown you the new No-homework King!"

Howie's face turned red.
It was as red as an apple. As
red as a fire engine. As red as
rocket flames.

"There really is a dragon
and I can prove it!"

7

DRAGON HUNTING

"Be very quiet," Eddie whispered. "We're hunting dragons." He pretended to lasso a dragon.

It was early the next morning and they were waiting in the woods for Howie's dragon to show up.

Melody tossed a make-believe net over the fake dragon. "Look out dragon, here we come," she said.

"I hope it's a nice dragon," Liza said. She was using her backpack as a shield to protect herself from imaginary dragon flames.

"Shhh," Howie said. "It's almost time."

The four kids dumped their backpacks on the ground and stared through the trees at the sky.

"It's CREEPY in the woods," Liza said. "It's full of spiders and bats and..."

"DRAGONS!" Howie finished.

The kids waited and waited.
They waited so long that they
each started daydreaming.

Eddie's tummy growled.
Thinking of pancakes had made
him hungry.

"Shhh," Howie said.

The growling came again.

"Be quiet," Howie told
Eddie.

Eddie gulped. "That
wasn't me."

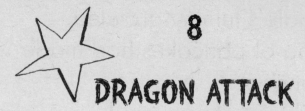

8

DRAGON ATTACK

Howie looked at Melody. Melody looked at Eddie. Eddie looked at Liza. Liza covered her eyes.

Suddenly, a shadow fell over the kids.

Overhead, a tree limb creaked. It groaned.

Then it SNAPPED! The limb fell to the ground with a shower of leaves.

"AHHHHH!" the kids screamed.

AHHHAH!

They did the only thing they could think of.

Howie ran right.

Melody ran left.

Eddie ran straight.

Liza stood frozen in her tracks.

They crashed into
one another and
ended up in a pile
of tangled arms
and legs.

"We're being
attacked by a
homework-eating
dragon!" Liza yelled.

"Not if I can help it,"
Eddie said.

He jumped up to fight
the dragon.
But when
Eddie looked
up, the sky
was empty.

9

MATH FOR BREAKFAST

"Which way did the dragon go?" Howie asked.

Melody helped Liza up from the ground. Twigs stuck out of their hair. The knees of their jeans were torn. Mud caked their sweatshirts.

"What dragon?" Melody asked. "I didn't see anything."

What dragon?

Howie looked at Melody like she had a carrot for a nose. "The dragon that almost ate us," he told her.

Melody put her hands on her hips. "There was no dragon. You've been making all this up so that you wouldn't get into trouble for not having your homework."

"I'm not making it up," Howie said. "Besides, I have my homework in my backpack."

Howie pointed to the spot where they had dropped their school things. There was only one problem. The backpacks were gone.

"Uh-oh," Eddie said. "Who took our homework?" Liza squealed.

"It was the dragon," Howie said. "He just ate our math for breakfast!"

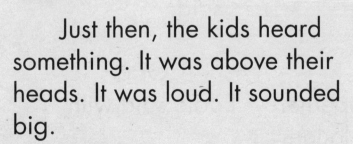

Just then, the kids heard something. It was above their heads. It was loud. It sounded big.

Very big.

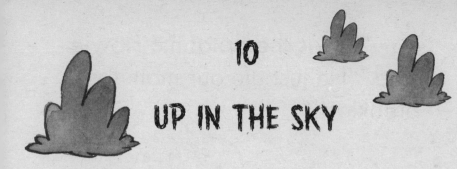

10

UP IN THE SKY

For just a minute, the sky turned as black as night.

"What was that?" Liza yelled.

"It could have been a low-flying plane," Melody said.

"Or a superhero," Eddie said with a laugh.

Liza looked up at the sky.
"Maybe it was just a flock of
big birds."

Howie shook his head.
"It was the dragon."

Just then, Eddie saw
something on the ground. It
was round and it sparkled.
He reached down to pick it up.
"What's this?" he asked.

"It's only a leaf," Melody said.

Eddie held it up so that the sun shone on it.

"That's no leaf," Howie said. "It's a scale. A dragon scale."

11

DRAGON CAVE

On Saturday morning, the four friends met on the path that led into the woods.

"We have the entire day to look," Howie said. "I'm going to prove that there is a homework-eating dragon living right here."

Liza looked into the woods. "Where do dragons hide?"

Howie held up a book about dragons. "It says here, 'dragons hide in caves and watch over their treasure.'"

Eddie suddenly got excited. He pushed Howie's book aside.

"You can keep your books. I want the treasure."

"Where should we start looking?" Melody asked.

Just then, they heard a sound in the leaves.

Howie darted behind a tree. Liza hid behind a rock. Eddie climbed up a tree trunk. Melody dived into a bush.

12

KNIGHT IN SHINING ARMOR

A man walked by on the path. He was dressed in silver. Silver shoes. Silver pants. Silver jacket. He even had on silver glasses and a silver bag on his shoulder.

"Who's that?" Eddie asked after the man disappeared down the path.

"I know," Howie said, flipping open his book to a picture. "He's a dragon-hunting knight!"

"He doesn't look like a knight," Eddie pointed out.

Melody nodded. "Knights wore suits of armor, not pants and jackets."

KLONK

KLONK

"But they did spend lots of time hunting dragons," Howie said as he rolled his eyes. "Anyway, knights of today wouldn't wear the same stuff they did long ago," he added.

"Why would a knight be creeping through these woods?" Liza asked.

"To find the dragon," Eddie said matter-of-factly.

"The poor dragon," Liza said. She looked ready to cry. "He didn't hurt anybody."

"Come on," Howie said.
"We have to follow the knight.
Maybe he'll lead us to the
dragon's cave."

The four friends followed
the dragon hunter until they
came upon a small cave. The
man crept up to the cave. He
had something big and silver
in his hands.

Liza dashed forward.
"Stop!" she screamed.

The man in silver ducked.
The cave exploded as something
crashed out of it.

"Look out!" Howie
screamed. "We're about to
be dragon toast!"
They all hit the ground and
covered their heads.

13
DRAGON HUNTER?

Swoosh-swish-swoosh! Melody saw the glitter of shiny scales.

Whomp-whomp-whomp! Howie heard the flutter of powerful wings.

Flip-flop-flip! Liza spotted a spiked tail.

Snort-snort-snort! Eddie thought he saw smoke. And then it was all gone.

The man in silver jumped up from the ground. "You scared him away!" he told Liza. "Why?"

"I was saving him from you," Liza said. "I thought you were going to hurt him."

"I wouldn't hurt him. I was just going to take his picture." The man held up a big camera.

"The giant-scaled albatross from the Dragonian Island is very rare. It's thought to be the smartest bird alive. I've been following

this bird for ten years. Now I have to start hunting for him all over again!"

With that, the man took his camera and crashed through the woods after the albatross.

14
TREASURE

"So it wasn't a dragon after all?" Liza asked.

"It was only a bird?" Melody asked.

"There wasn't any treasure?" Eddie kicked at a rock. "We were dumb to think that a dragon would like homework."

"Don't be so sure," Howie said as he looked inside the cave. "You might be wrong," he said. "Maybe dragons DO eat homework."

The kids peeked inside the dim cave. Scales of different colors lay on the floor of the cave.

"What's that?" Liza asked, pointing to a big pile.

"The dragon's treasure," Howie said.

"TREASURE!" Eddie cheered and ran inside.

Liza and Melody followed Eddie into the cave. It was too dark in the cave to see what the treasure was. They stood there, blinking in the dark for a few minutes.

Then Melody and Liza helped Howie carry everything out into the sunlight.

Eddie took
one look at the
pile and threw
his baseball cap
on the ground.
His face turned
as red as his hair.

There, piled on the ground,
were backpacks, books, and a
week's worth of homework.

"That's no treasure," Eddie
snapped.

"Yes, it is," Howie said with a grin. "Books and homework help us learn. That's the best treasure a kid, or a dragon, could ever have!"